Angelina of Italy

BY MAYA ANGELOU
ILLUSTRATED BY LIZZY ROCKWELL

A Random House PICTUREBACK® Book

RANDOM HOUSE 🏠 NEW YORK

Text copyright © 2004 by Maya Angelou. Illustrations copyright © 2004 by Lizzy Rockwell. All rights reserved under International and Pan-American Copyright Conventions. Published in the United States by Random House Children's Books, a division of Random House, Inc., New York, and simultaneously in Canada by Random House of Canada Limited, Toronto.
www.randomhouse.com/kids
Library of Congress Cataloging-in-Publication Data
Angelou, Maya. Angelina of Italy / by Maya Angelou ; illustrated by Lizzy Rockwell. — 1st ed.   p.   cm. — (Random House pictureback)
SUMMARY: Angelina, who loves pizza, becomes very concerned when she learns about the Leaning Tower of Pisa, which she believes is made of pizza.
ISBN 0-375-82832-X (trade) — ISBN 0-375-92832-4 (lib. bdg.)
[1. Pizza—Fiction. 2. Leaning Tower (Pisa, Italy)—Fiction. 3. Italy—Fiction.] I. Rockwell, Lizzy, ill. II. Title. III. Series.
PZ7.A5833An 2004 [E]—dc22 2003017636
Printed in the United States of America   First Edition   10 9 8 7 6 5 4 3 2
PICTUREBACK, RANDOM HOUSE, and the Random House colophon are registered trademarks of Random House, Inc.

When I was a little girl,

I looked around at my world.

It was small, so was I.

Then my world began to grow

With each child I came to know.

Now I try,

Now I dare

To make a new friend

Everywhere.

Let me tell you about my friend Angelina. She is a little girl who lives in Italy. *Angelina* means "little angel." Most of the time she *is* an angel, but sometimes she gets a mischievous twinkle in her eye—which is just what she had the day she told me this story. And now I will tell it to you. . . .

Angelina was a friendly, happy little girl. She liked to say *"Ciao!"* to all her neighbors and friends as they passed by her window. (You pronounce *ciao* "chow." It's a very useful word that means "hello" and "goodbye.")

Angelina loved pizza—all kinds of pizza. Pepperoni pizza. Vegetable pizza. Insalata pizza. Even sardine pizza! She loved pizza so much that her sister, Annalisa, called her "Patty Pizza," which Angelina didn't care for!

One night, Angelina and her whole family were sitting down to dinner. Angelina had a big family! There were her mama and papa, her twin baby brothers, Franco and Fredo, her big sister, Annalisa, and her Uncle Armando. Mama had to call Uncle Armando to the table twice because he was playing the guitar and singing loudly.

Angelina's mama had two platters in her hands—one heaped high with steaming pasta with meat sauce and basil, and the other with a delicious pepper-bacon-mushroom-meatball pizza—just for Angelina!

"Mangia!" said Mama. "Eat!"

When Uncle Armando wasn't singing, he was telling stories. In between bites of pasta, he told the family about the Leaning Tower of Pisa. It was very tall, and every year it leaned farther and farther, until one day surely it would fall.

"A leaning tower of pizza?" cried Angelina. This was the worst news she had ever heard!

Angelina imagined a tower made of delicious, saucy pizza pies rising as tall as the church steeple down the street. The Leaning Tower of Pizza leaned farther and farther. If it fell over, no one would ever have a chance to eat it! Especially her!

"Don't worry, darlinghissima," said Angelina's mama. "The Tower is made of marble and concrete and metal." But Angelina didn't believe it.

The next morning, Angelina curled up in the window seat. Friends and neighbors waved hello, but she didn't call out *"Ciao!"* like she usually did. She just couldn't get the Leaning Tower of Pizza out of her mind.

Papa gave Angelina a squeeze. "Come, my little angel. We're going for a ride."

The whole family squeezed into their little car—Angelina, Mama, Papa, Franco, Fredo, Annalisa, and even Uncle Armando. As they drove off, he began to sing. *"Canta! Canta!"* he demanded. So everyone sang along with him the whole trip—except for Angelina.

Papa drove to the next town, which was called . . . guess what? Pisa! A tall tower rose up before them. It didn't stand straight. It definitely leaned toward the ground! The Leaning Tower of Pizza! As she stared up at it, Angelina was sure she could see the mozzarella dripping off it. She began to sniffle.

Closer and closer they came. By now, big tears were rolling down Angelina's cheeks. Papa stopped the car, and before anyone could stop her, Angelina jumped out and ran toward the tower. There were ropes and gates around it. A stern man stood guard at the entrance.

Angelina ducked under the ropes. *"Ferma!"* shouted the guard. "Stop!" And reaching down, he scooped her up in his arms.

The whole family—Mama, Papa, Franco, Fredo, Annalisa, and even Uncle Armando—came running and yelling.

For the first time, Angelina got a good look at the Tower. She was so near, she could almost reach out and touch it. And now she could see with her own eyes that the Tower was made of marble and concrete and metal. There wasn't a piece of pepperoni or drippy mozzarella in sight!

"It's not made of pizza!" she whispered. The guard scolded Angelina for running under the ropes, but he couldn't help but laugh.

When Mama explained to the guard about Angelina's
little misunderstanding, the guard laughed even harder.
  "Everyone knows how much Angelina *loves* her pizza!"
said Uncle Armando.

"Patty Pizza! Patty Pizza!" singsonged Franco and Fredo. The guard chuckled. Soon Angelina was smiling, and her whole family began to laugh—Mama, Papa, Franco, Fredo, Annalisa, and Uncle Armando. Even Angelina. Somehow that nickname didn't bother her anymore!

"Let's all go home and eat a great big pizza pie with everything!" said Angelina's papa. And that is *just* what they did.

Angelina's story made me laugh. I hope it made you laugh, too. *Ciao*, my friend.